THE INVINCIBLE
TONY
SPEARS

HODDER CHILDREN'S BOOKS

First published in Great Britain in 2018 by Hodder and Stoughton

10 9 8 7 6 5 4 3 2 1

ISBN 978 1 444 91972 1

Printed and bound by CPI Group (UK) Ltd, Croydon, CR0 4YY

The paper and board used in this book are made from wood from responsible sources.

Hodder Children's Books
An imprint of Hachette Children's Group
Part of Hodder and Stoughton
Carmelite House
50 Victoria Embankment
London EC4Y 0DZ
An Hachette UK Company
www.hachette.co.uk

www.hachettechildrens.co.uk

THE INVINCIBLE
TONY SPEARS
LOST IN SPACE

Neal Layton

Hodder
Children's
Books

1. FROM HERE TO THERE

Lots of things changed when Tony became a big brother.

One minute Tara was in his mum's tummy, and the next she was there with them in their flat. His little sister: blinking, wriggling, gurgling ... and crying – she seemed to do lots of that.

He hadn't had time to think about it at first, there had been so much to do when she was born, but now several months on Tony realised that things would never be quite the same again. Their flat had become a very busy place, and he desperately needed some time alone.

Luckily, Tony had his very own spaceship, the *Invincible,* a type 1AA vessel capable of planetary, galactic and other forms of dimensional travel. Once Tony was on board the spaceship he was totally safe, and he could zoom about the universe wherever he wished. The trouble was that to get on board, he had to press the secret button hidden in his kitchen

cupboard.

THE KITCHEN CUPBOARD

THE SIGN AND THE BUTTON

DAMPERS

The button activated the hyper-lift to the underground bunker where the *Invincible* was kept, but now with baby Tara around, there always seemed to be someone in the kitchen. Tony hadn't been able to fly for months.

That afternoon, Tony's friend Chandra was coming over. Chandra was Tony's best girl friend at school – although she wasn't a girlfriend, just a friend who was a girl. She didn't know about the *Invincible*, but sometimes Tony wondered if she suspected there was something different about him.

The clock in the lounge said 4.15 p.m., which meant Chandra was due to arrive in an hour. It didn't give Tony long, but baby Tara and his mum were asleep upstairs. The kitchen was empty – an hour zooming in space was better than nothing!

Tony wore his communicator on his wrist. It looked a bit like a watch, and it meant he could keep in touch with his spaceship, even when he was not on board.

Tony whispered into his communicator, 'Computer, are you there?'

'Affirmative, Master Spears.'

'Listen, I'm going to try and launch. I really need to buzz round the universe for a bit. Are you ready for a quick take-off?'

'Certainly, Master Spears, all systems are fully functional, and my dilithium crystals are completely charged.'

'Ace! I'm going to tiptoe into the kitchen now ...'

Tony closed the kitchen door behind him

and crept his way over to the cupboard where the secret button was hidden. He gently opened the door, and moved several packs of nappies to one side to reveal the button, but just as he was about to press it, there was a crashing noise in the lounge and the kitchen door flew open …

WAH! WAH! WAH!

It was Mum. 'Ahh, Tony, brilliant. You must have known — what a good big brother you are! Throw me another pack of nappies, will you?'

Tony groaned. Not again. He loved being a big brother, but sometimes he just needed to do big brother things, like flying spaceships!

'And listen,' continued his mum, 'Chandra will be here soon. Why don't you go and tidy Tara's toys away in the lounge. They seem to be all over the place again.'

'Um, OK,' mumbled Tony, as he sloped back into the lounge. Pushing the door open revealed a sea of plastic toys scattered across the floor. And there, on the floor amongst them, were the broken remains of his space rocket model.

Tony was very proud of his space rocket model. It was a scaled-down replica of a Saturn 5 moon rocket. It had taken him months to build and paint, and there it was, on the floor, in bits.

'MUUUM!' shouted Tony. 'Tara has knocked over my space rocket model!'

Tony's mum was in the middle of changing Tara's nappy. It didn't seem to be going well.

'Look, Tony, if you leave things lying around she will want to play with them. I told you to put it high up on the bookshelf.

'I'm sure it can be mended. If you pick up the pieces whilst you're tidying Tara's toys I'll see what I can do later,' she said.

Tony made his way back into the lounge. Putting his broken rocket to one side, he picked up toys, bricks, rattles and shakers and threw them into the toy box beside the playmat.

Suddenly, there was a muffled buzz coming from his wrist. All the toy tidying must have made his communicator slip. Readjusting the strap, he whispered, 'Computer, is that you? Sorry, Mum's in the kitchen now, so I can't fly ...'

'Affirmative, Master Spears.'

And then Tony stopped. The toy tidying had given him an idea.

'Computer. Are you still there?'

'Affirmative, Master Spears.'

'Listen, is there any other way I can get on

board? I mean this button and hyper-lift is all very well, but with the kitchen so busy all the time I never seem to be able to press it.'

'Certainly, Master Spears, I can teleport you.'

'Teleport?' said Tony.

'It is one of the many functions of your communicator ... Master Spears, you really must pay more attention when I explain things to you.

'To reiterate, although your communicator's main function is for you to stay in contact with me, it has many other modes – including flight control, biostatistical analysis, dimension warping, and the aforementioned teleportation.'

'OK, thanks, Computer. Just tell me what I need to do.'

'Firstly, close the door to the lounge. Next stand on exactly the coordinates I specify. I suggest you stand in the middle of Tara's round playmat, which happens to be the exact same dimensions as the radius of teleportation. Then on a count of three I will teleport you on board the spaceship. It's very simple when done properly.'

'OK. I'm ready,' said Tony.

1, 2,

For a split second Tony felt like his insides were being stretched out really long and thin like an elastic band, and then – *snap* – he was back in one piece again, on the bridge of the *Invincible*.

'Wow!' exclaimed Tony.

'Good afternoon, Master Spears. From your startled expression I assume that was the first time you have teleported? I believe it is a rather strange sensation for lifeforms to experience.'

'Um, yes. It was a bit strange but I'm OK.

C'mon, let's go, we haven't got long!'

And within seconds, Tony was flying through the clouds, through the stratosphere and beyond, into star-speckled outer space …WOOOO HOOOO!

2. CONTACT?

'Boy, have I missed this!' grinned Tony, as planets and stars zipped by the viewing screen.

'Master Spears, where shall I set course for today?'

'I'm not sure, Computer, let's just carry on going this way.'

'That looks like an interesting planet, Master Spears, shall I head there? Or what about this abandoned space-station off the starboard bow?'

'Oh, I dunno. I just want to do something different …'

'Perhaps we could visit the Gabba-Gabba system. We haven't been there for a while, and I do like interfacing with their cyber-bots.'

'But we've done all those things before,' replied Tony.

'Wait, Master Spears; something is speaking to us across all frequencies.'

'Computer, please patch it through to the bridge so I can hear it.'

'boo goo.'

'Computer, what was that? Was it a message?'

'I'm not sure, Master Spears.'

'boo-boo.'

'I'm analysing it now, Tony.'

'boo boo, baaaaaa!'

'Is it an alien, Computer?'

'baaa gaaa gooo grrrrgle!'

'Perhaps an unknown lifeform trying to contact us, trying to communicate with us?' continued Tony.

'I am narrowing its point of origin now. It's coming from the Orion spur of the Milky Way galaxy ... location ... planet Earth.'

'Earth?! You mean my planet? Computer, there's something familiar about that voice ...'

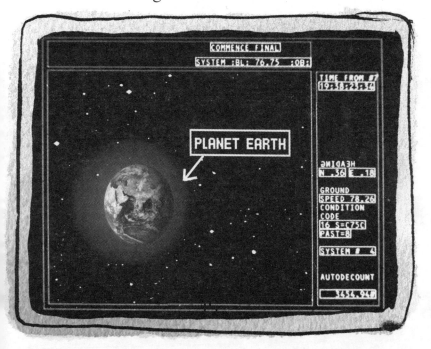

'I have pinpointed its source and analysed the voice pattern. It is in fact coming from your house. Tony, it is your sister.'

'Tara?'

'Yes. She is in your kitchen and must have your communicator. I'm sensing large amounts of humidity which would suggest she is enjoying chewing it.'

Tony looked at his wrist. His communicator was not there. He must have left it behind when he was teleporting.

'Computer, change of plan. I think we'd better not go anywhere today. I need to get home super quick before Tara presses any other—'

Suddenly the *Invincible* started to lurch violently from side to side.

'Buttons … aghhh!'

3. REMOTE CONTROL

'Compuuuuttttteerrrrr, what's haaaapppennnning?!'

'Tara has engaged the remote controls on your communicator, and is now at the helm of the *Invincible*, but it would appear she does not know how to fly an interstellar super-mega-spaceship.'

'Computer, please engage manual controls,' instructed Tony.

'I'm sorry, Tony. I'm afraid I can't do that. Your communicator has priority. Until baby Tara disengages remote controls she is at the helm of the ship.'

'But she's a baby … !'

'She might be a baby, but nevertheless, whilst in possession of your communicator, she is in control of us. Every time she presses ↑ we fly up, every time she presses ↓ we fly down, and every time she presses ↱ we spin round and round and round and round and round.'

Meanwhile, back on planet Earth, in Tony's house, Tara had crawled forwards to her toy box and tipped it out on the floor. There were assorted squashy balls, plastic bricks and dangly rattly things, but the communicator, with its flashing lights and buttons, was by far the most interesting thing within reach.

After thoroughly chewing it with her gums, she began to investigate it with her fingers. Every time she pushed one of the buttons, it flashed pretty colours and made a funny noise.

Meanwhile back in outer space, Tony was spinning around violently.

'Computerrrrrr, aghhhhhhh! Make it stop!'

Back on planet Earth, Tara had found a brand new button to press. And immediately the *Invincible* stopped its erratic spinning course.

'Tony, Tara has disengaged remote control on your communicator.'

I don't believe it, thought Tony. *I'm zillions of space miles away from home and Tara still seems to interrupt my games.*

'Computer, set course for home, at super-duper speed.'

'Affirmative, Master Spears.'

4. MICRO MACHINE

The universe is a very big place. So big that sometimes, even travelling at super-duper speed doesn't seem fast enough.

'Computer, how long until touchdown?'

'Entering Earth's atmosphere now, Tony. Opening landing hatch. Reversing landing thrusters.'

But as they got nearer to home, Tony noticed something was wrong.

'What? My house, it seems different; it's way too big. Abort landing!'

Lights started flashing all over the control panel in front of Tony.

'I think I know what's happening. Your house isn't big; it's us, we have become smaller. Tara has engaged the MICRO ↔ function and is repeatedly pressing it. We are becoming miniaturised. We are now small enough to enter your house via your bedroom window.'

'OK, Computer, let's go in through my bedroom window then. We can zoom through my room and down the stairs to where Tara is. We need to get my communicator back before my sister presses anything else.'

'Right, now along the hall – watch it, there's Mum!' said Tony.

'Tony, Tara is still pressing the MICRO button. We are now the size of a small bird.'

'Aghh. What's that?' screamed Tony's mum as they whizzed past her head. 'Chris, CHRIS! Come quickly, there's a bird in the house. It's gone into the lounge.'

Chris was Tara's dad.

'My goodness, that's not a bird; it could be a large moth though, or some kind of hornet,' said Chris.

'A hornet!' exclaimed Tony's mum. 'Quick, get it out of here now. It could sting little Tara!'

'There it is. I'll get it with this rolled-up newspaper,' said Chris.

'Tony, she is still pressing the ↔ button. We are now the size of a hornet.'

'Try not to swat it though, Chris. Just shoo it out, will you?' said Tony's mum.

'We are still shrinking, and are now the size of a bluebottle.'

'Tara, put that down, will you. That's not yours, it's Tony's.'

As Tony's mum scooped Tara up into her arms, Tara dropped the communicator and the lights on Tony's control panel stopped flashing so wildly.

'We've stopped shrinking. Thank goodness for that. Right, Computer, can you fly us in close so I can grab my communicator?'

All of a sudden Tony's house, where he would normally feel nice and safe, felt very dangerous.

'Chris, CHRIS, it's that hornet thing again. It's trying to sting Tara!'

'Don't worry, it just looks like a fly or some sort of small flying insect,' Chris replied.

As Tony came in to grab the communicator, Chris swiped with his newspaper, missing the *Invincible*, but flicking the communicator across the room.

'Woah, that was close!' exclaimed Tony.

'Tony, we have a new problem. When Chris knocked the communicator with his newspaper it pressed the MACRO ⇕ button.'

'What does that do?'

'It enlarges our size, Tony. We are now expanding.'

'Great, I mean we want to be big again, don't we?'

'Yes, but in forty-five seconds we will reach normal size, and we are currently in your lounge, which is not large enough to accommodate an interstellar spacecraft.'

5. BIGGER AND BIGGER

'Destination outer space … NOW!'

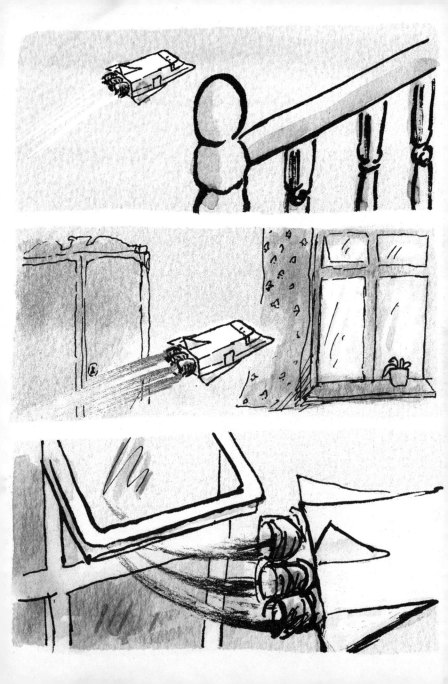

'We're going to make it out the window.'

As they flew up through the clouds, the computer announced: **'Reaching normal size ... NOW but until the STOP button is pressed we will continue expanding.'**

As they passed beyond Mars, the computer announced: **'We are now larger than planet Earth and still growing.'**

'When will this stop?' asked Tony.

'I'm not sure. Nobody has ever tried this before.

'We are now larger than the sun ... our size is beginning to have an effect on the orbits of the solar system. We must remove ourselves to a safe distance or the results could be catastrophic for planet Earth.'

Meanwhile, back on planet Earth in Tony's house, Tony's mum was with Tara, who had just noticed the funny toy she'd been playing with before. She crawled across the floor towards it. She tried to get it to make the pretty lights and sounds it made before, but it kept making an angry beeping noise.

'Tara, what have you got in your mouth now?' said Tony's mum.

'Now that's *not* yours, is it? I do wish Tony wouldn't leave his toys around. And you've been pressing buttons on it too. Now how do I get this awful alarm to stop?

'Is it this button?'

'Or this?'

'Perhaps if I just press everything …'

'Thank goodness for that. I couldn't bear

any more of that awful noise! I'll give it a clean
and put it up here, out of harm's way to dry.'

Meanwhile, somewhere in outer space …

**'Tony, the MACRO feature has been
switched OFF. We will soon be normal super-
mega-spaceship size again.'**

'Thank goodness for that,' said Tony.

Slumped in his seat, he felt like he had been on the biggest, wildest fairground ride in the universe, and he probably had.

'Please Computer, destination Earth, my house. I've had enough of this. I want control of my life back! Let's get that communicator before anything else happens.'

5. DOING THE TIMEWARP

So for the second time that afternoon, Tony came in to land back on planet Earth. And for the second time that day, planet Earth looked, well, different.

Looking out of the window of the *Invincible*, Tony couldn't see any streets, or houses, but only volcanoes, swamps and jungles. Suddenly a huge head reared up from behind a palm tree and snapped at the *Invincible* with mighty jaws.

'Tony, we have another problem ...'

'You're telling me – Computer, you've taken me to the wrong planet, this isn't Earth.'

'I'm afraid this *is* Earth, Tony, as it was around 100 million years ago, in the early Cretaceous period. I neglected to notice that when your mum wiped down your communicator, she accidentally engaged the

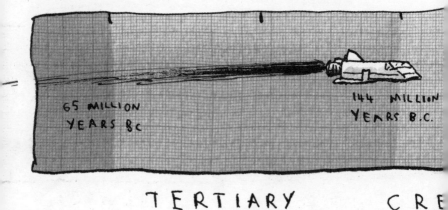

65 MILLION YEARS BC

144 MILLION YEARS B.C.

TERTIARY   CRE

Time Manipulation setting ◄◄'

'You mean we've gone back in time?'

'Going back, Tony. We're still travelling back in time, and at an ever increasing rate.'

On the viewing screen, Tony could see jungles receding, and then flattening out and filling with water, lots of water.

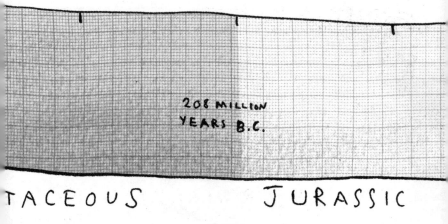

208 MILLION YEARS B.C.

TACEOUS   JURASSIC

'There's nowhere to land.'

'Correct, Master Spears. We're now entering approximately 500 million years ago, the Cambrian era, when planet Earth was more than 85% water. The only life present is sea sponges, ammonites and larger creatures, trilobites and anomalocaris. This really is most fascinating, Tony. We are watching the development of life on Earth backwards, at breakneck speed.

'The universe is shrinking. Please take your seat, Master Spears. If this continues we will eventually enter a singularity.'

'What do you mean?'

'We are heading back in time towards the BIG BANG, towards the beginning of the universe itself. Singularity in 30, 29, 28,

27, 26, 25, 24, 23, 22 ...

'What shall we do, Computer? Help!'

'I'm afraid there is nothing we can do. We just have to hope the *Invincible* will survive this.'

Hearing this made Tony glad he was on board the *Invincible*. It had been given that name because it was, as its name implied, totally invincible. When Tony was on board, as long as all windows were shut, he was totally safe. And as they headed backwards towards the Big Bang, this theory was about to undergo the ultimate test.

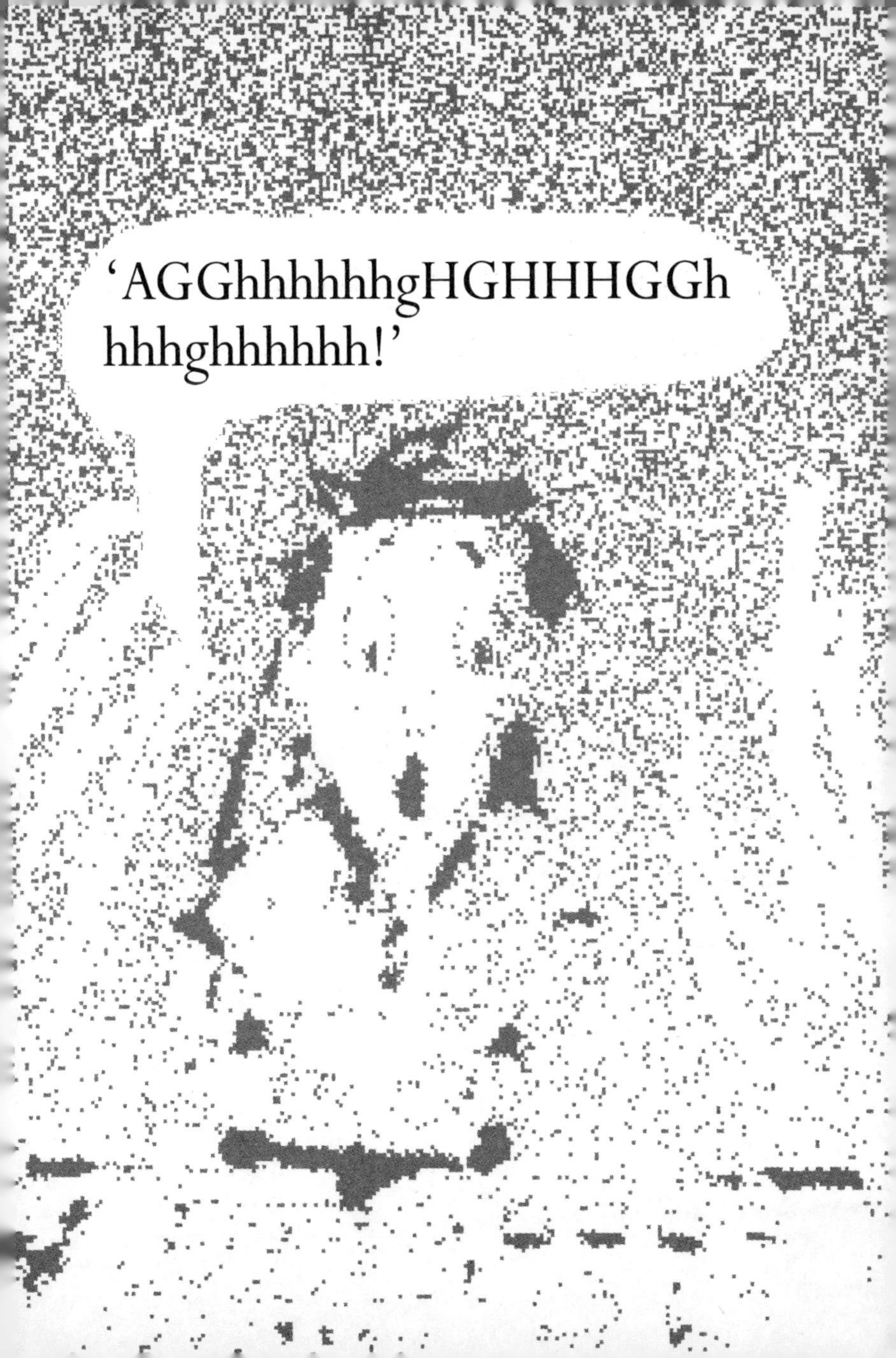
'AGGhhhhhhgHGHHHGGh
hhhghhhhhh!'

Then everything went normal again. It was kind of like pressing rewind on a TV, then pausing, and pressing play again.

Tony sat in his chair sweating. He wiped his brow.

'I never ever want to do that again! Right, now please can we go home? I have had enough of being shrunk, stretched, spun and all the rest of it. I want to go home and have my tea, like normal children do.'

'Master Spears, I'm afraid something rather unexpected has happened.'

'What do you mean?'

'Take a look at the viewing screen, Tony, and I'll explain.'

'Computer, it doesn't seem to be working. There's nothing there. It's bright white.'

EXTERIOR VIEW | LIVE

Tony zoomed in on a few areas.

'There's nothing, not even the darkness of space, just some sort of smudge on the screen. It must be broken—'

'I'm afraid it's not broken, Tony. There appears to be no stars, or planets, because there are no stars or planets here. In fact there is almost nothing at all.'

'What do you mean, nothing … and where is HERE? Computer, where are we? What's happened?'

6. ANOTHER DIMENSION

'I'm afraid travelling back in time beyond the origin of our universe seems to have popped us into a different dimension.'

Tony stared blankly back at the computer screen.

'Let me explain ...

'You live on planet Earth, which is in something you call The Universe.

'But that universe is only one of many universes that exist side by side. Kind of like neighbours you never meet. You know they live next door, and occasionally you hear them through the wall, but you don't see them. There are actually kazillions of universes.

A PARALLEL UNIVERSE

AND ANOTHER PARALLEL UNIVERSE

ZILLIONS OF OTHER ONES!

OUR UNIVERSE

YET ANOTHER PARALLEL UNIVERSE

ANOTHER PARALLEL UNIVERSE

'And so travelling back in time, beyond the origin of our universe, seems to have sent us into a parallel universe in another dimension.'

'But I don't want to be here. I want to be back where I belong, home. In fact, I *need* to get home, it's tea time and I'm hungry!'

'Don't worry, Master Spears, the *Invincible* can create food for you for many years until my dilithium crystals run down.'

'I want normal Earth food. Can't Tara or anyone just get my communicator and press

▶▶ to whizz us back through time to where we left?'

'I'm afraid that won't work, Tony. Now we have popped into another dimension I am unable to communicate with our universe. We are completely cut off.

'If there is any way for us to get back, we will have to work it out ourselves. But I have to tell you, Tony, we have ended up in a dimension which is almost entirely empty, so our chances are extremely slim.'

'What do you mean – I'm stuck here?'

'At present, Master Spears, yes. And probably for ever.'

'Wait … Computer, you said there was *almost* nothing here …'

'Correct, Master Spears. Although we

can't see anything, there is matter out there and I calculate that I will be able to land, and it will support your weight.'

'OK, Computer. Bring us in to land. Perhaps I can find some answers outside the spaceship, and maybe find a way home.'

And so the *Invincible* landed in one of
the strangest places it had ever been to. The
ship hovered, unfolded its landing feet and
then touched down. Tony heard the gangplank

extending down to the ground, and with a hiss-clunk, the hull doors opened and Tony began to walk bravely out.

'**Good luck, Master Spears,**' called out the computer, as Tony passed through the doors.

'**And remember not to stray far. Without your communicator, we have no means of staying in contact.**'

7. WHERE NOW?

Of course Tony had seen the images on the viewing screen but nothing could prepare him for the actual thing. It was like being in a very

pristine white room where everything was white, very white. Although there didn't seem to be any sky, or horizon, his feet seemed to find solid ground with each step.

Tony took a last look at the *Invincible* and
began to walk slowly away.

He glanced over his shoulder every now and
then to see it getting smaller and smaller, until
he could hardly see it at all.

By now with all this walking he was beginning to feel hungry and thirsty. He guessed it must time for his after-school snack. Any minute now at home Chandra would be arriving. His mum would be wondering where he was.

Tony sat down to rest. He'd craved a bit of time on his own but not this.

Tony started to notice a fruity smell, and with a high-pitched shriek, like someone blowing a recorder hard, a strange plant appeared. It was like a little tree, except its

bark was red, and its leaves were orange.

Dangling from its branches were green ball-like

fruits, covered in white spots.

With two or three more recorder-like
shrieks, more plants appeared. At least, Tony
thought they were plants. Some had round
green spotty fruits, and some had long red
stripy ones.

Tony walked towards the round green spotty plant and sniffed. They not only looked green and spotty, but they actually smelt of green and white spots too. Tony realised he definitely was hungry.

He reached out to touch them. They were smooth to the touch, with fine bristles, almost like fur. Suddenly one of the green spotty-fruit-things twisted from the branch and dropped into his hand.

It had a good weight to it. Sniffing it again, Tony realised that this was definitely where the green spotty fruity smell was coming from. And before he knew what he was doing, he bit into it … just a little, to test it.

At first it tasted delicious, but when Tony bit into it harder, suddenly the taste went very sour. So he spat it out on to the ground. Yuk!

Tony felt overcome with sadness. He was alone, alone in some unknown place. Everything was different, and he didn't know what to do. He could feel tears welling up. It felt like his whole insides had been turned upside down.

But NO! He wasn't going to cry. He wasn't a baby … and then he thought of Tara, his little baby sister, so interested in everything, and so full of hope. And her big gummy grin. Tears were coming now, he couldn't stop them …

Through his tears Tony began to notice another noise, like the wailing of an injured animal.

'Booooooooooooo!'

'Hooooooooooooooo!'

Tony wiped away his tears. A group of misshapen balls rolled up to him, and with the

sound of porridge bubbling each one plopped
into a little blue pile, with eyes.

No matter how strange these wailing
companions looked, Tony was glad of the
company, and perhaps, just perhaps, they could
help him.

'Um, hello,' said Tony.

'**Blurp, blurp, bleep,**' bleeped the little mounds.

'Sorry to cry like that,' said Tony, 'I'm sad because I need help, you see. I'm lost. Can you tell me where I am? I need to get home.'

'Bleep. Blep. Blep. Blep. Bloop.'

At this more balls rolled up, popping into pimple-mounds and forming a circle around him.

'Can you help me please?'

'Blurp, blurp,

Blurp, blurp,

Blurp, blurp.'

The circle of little mounds started closing towards Tony, picking him up from the ground and whisking him away like a football team carrying their mascot.

8. DR POLIVOKS

By now the mounds were moving Tony at quite
a considerable speed.

'Where are you taking me? Stop, I said STOP!'

'Bloop, bloop. Blep.'

When the mounds did eventually stop, they did so very suddenly and Tony flew through the air, landing in a huge thicket of striped-spotty plants.

'OW!' he exclaimed.

As Tony landed, he could see that beside the thicket, there was a little old man busily picking the green and white spotty fruit things, putting them into a bag over his shoulder. Beside him, lots of the little blue mounds were helping.

The man had a bald head and was wearing a big pair of glasses and a white coat. His pockets were brimming with bits of wire, strange-looking tools, pens and all manner of weird and wonderful-looking instruments. Tony also noticed he was wearing odd socks.

'Oh, my. What do we have here?' said the man. 'A boy? You wouldn't be a human boy by any chance would you? You certainly look like one, though it's been a long time since I've seen one – and your ears look a bit big.'

'Um, yes, I am. My name is Tony Spears. Where am I?'

'Well hello, Tony. Welcome to another dimension. I'm Dr Polivoks, or you can call me Dr P for short.'

As Dr Polivoks spoke, several of the blue mounds rolled themselves together into a sort of chair. Dr P sat down and began talking …

'It happened like this … You see, I was

a young, ambitious scientist, living in your

universe, or 'The Universe' as we used to call it.

'I'd been exploring the possibility of time travel, and for many years had been constructing a time machine with the intention of sending a piece of cheese back in time. I thought I'd start with one piece of cheese, then a slice, and then maybe a whole cheese. Imagine that, a whole cheese travelling back in time!

'So, I'd set up this experiment with a piece of cheddar, or was it emmental, and then what should happen but before I was ready, my assistant flicked the ACTIVATE switch with his tail.'

'Your assistant had a tail?' asked Tony.

'Of course he did. All cats have tails, don't they?

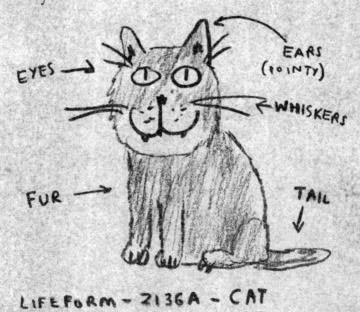

EYES →

EARS
(POINTY)

← WHISKERS

FUR →

TAIL
↓

LIFEFORM - 2136A - CAT

'Anyway, his tail flicked, the cheese went back in time, it was a success! But then something went wrong and it reappeared INSIDE my atomiser-air-bulb-array, causing a malfunction, and before you know it, bang! I'm here. Laboratory and all. Stuck in another dimension.'

'But wait, Dr Polivoks. You said you came here with your laboratory, and the experiment that sent you here. Where is all this stuff? There doesn't seem to be anything here.'

'In BLUE BLOO City of course,' said

Dr P, pointing up to the sky.

Tony looked up and there, hanging in the sky above them, at the most weird and wonderful angle, was a magnificent city.

'Wow!' exclaimed Tony. 'How do we get up there?'

'We walk of course, you can remember how to walk, can't you – you've been doing it since you were about one year old!'

And with that, the old man strode up, and into the air.

Tony tried to step up. His foot seemed to place itself in the air, and feel firm. He tried another step, and another …

9. BLUE BLOO CITY

It took a lot of concentration to walk up to
Blue Bloo City, but once Tony had the hang
of it, his mind began racing with questions.
He told Dr P all about his spaceship, and the
communicator, and his little sister Tara.

'Everything seems different here at first,
but you'll get used to it, Tony,' said Dr P. 'Look
at it this way. Your baby sister Tina …'

'She's called Tara.'

'Yes, Tina. Well, when she was born on Earth, she didn't know anything about anything. She had to learn what sounds are, what smells are, about hard things, soft things, loud things, quiet things. Every day is an adventure for her. She tries things out. She makes mistakes but she learns.

'So for the time being just think of
yourself as a big baby, having to learn all about
the new world you find yourself in.'

'But I'm not a big baby, I'm eight years old!' said Tony. 'I think I'd quite like to go home, really. You're a scientist so you must know how to get back.'

'Unfortunately, none of my experiments have ever worked out properly,' Dr P said sadly. 'Anyway, that's enough of all that talk. It'll set the Blue Bloos off crying and I never can stand that. Here we are at Blue Bloo City; you must be hungry ... follow me.'

Inside the city gates Tony's senses were hit with a kaleidoscopic carnival of colours, smells and sights.

'The food halls are this way. Now what shall we start with? Stripy fruits. Spotty fruits, make sure you eat the skins not the insides, their insides taste horrible.'

Something buzzed past Tony's ear, and Dr Polivoks's head.

Swatting the air, Dr P shouted, 'Shoo! No flies in the food halls!'

And grabbing a plate, he began walking around the food counters, filling it with strange fruits, vegetables, nuts and bread. Once the plate was piled high Dr P took a seat and gestured to Tony to do the same.

At the sight of all that 'food', Tony's tummy began to rumble.

'Go on, Tony, tuck in. I've already had my blunch. That's what they call it here. Blekky, that's breakfast. Blunch, that's lunch, and binglebunglebooboo. That's their word for tea. Always found that one hard to remember. You will of course have to learn Bloo Bloo, the language here ... but first things first, go on – eat.'

Tony eyeballed his plate. Nothing resembled anything he'd ever seen before. He began eating, but as soon as he bit into a curly whirly hoop, it popped, sending brown sauce all over his face and shirt.

Dr P looked at him. 'Looks like somebody's having a good lunch ... But oh

deary me, I didn't give you anything to eat
with.'

Dr P handed Tony a thin bendy stick. 'Permit me to demonstrate,' he said.

And with that he flicked several round things off his plate, up into the air and straight into his mouth.

Tony noticed all the Blue Bloos were doing the same, as if it was the most natural thing in the world.

Tony suddenly thought, *Perhaps this is what Tara feels like.*

The world must be a bewildering place to her. Full of new sights, sounds, smells. All she wants to

sense of it, to feel like she can join in and
be

Yes, thought Tony. *Now I'm a schoolboy, I think I know lots, but perhaps I might have a lot to learn from her.*

'Dr P, how come you know so much about this place?' asked Tony.

'Well, some of it I learnt, just like you. How to walk up. That balls bounce up, not down. That kind of thing. But when I arrived, I was lonely.

'So I built robots, and then I built a

machine to make robots, but something went a bit squiffy in the programming, and they started speaking their own language.'

'The Blue Bloos are robots?' asked Tony.

'Yes, all of them.'

are they all blue? And why do they

e time?'

Well, all I had in my lab was blue putty. The Blue Bloos copy. That's how they learn. So all the time they will be looking at me and now you, and seeing the things we do, and trying to do the same, and remembering. If you look sad and cry, they will too.'

Tony looked at one of the Blue Bloos. The Blue Bloo looked back at him.

'**Blep,**' it said.

'And of course I learn from them too.'

'That's Blue Bloo for hello, by the way,' whispered Dr P to Tony.

'Um, hello,' said Tony.

'**Bloop. Bloop,**' said the Blue Bloo.

'Dr P, can I see your time machine?'

'Yes, the Blue Bloos will lead the way.'

And for the first time since he'd arrived Tony had a glimmer of hope. If a time machine had got Dr P here, it must surely be able to take him back.

10. DR P'S LABORATORY

Tony followed the Blue Bloos and Dr P to an enormous pair of wobbly blue gates.

The Blue Bloos split into two groups and slowly began pushing the huge gates open to reveal what looked like a garden shed.

'My laboratory,' announced Dr. P proudly.

Tony's heart sank. He had been pinning all his hopes on this. Surely nothing inside a garden shed would get them home. *It's no wonder Dr Polivoks has been stuck here all this time*, he thought miserably.

But once Dr P had levered the rickety door open, and Tony peeped inside, his spirits heartened.

Inside, it was much larger than it appeared, and filled with piles of notes, bubbling test tubes, circuit boards, odd bits of

pipes and hundreds of clocks stacked up on top of one another. In the centre of the room was a large shiny silver egg, about the size of a small family car. There was a hole at the bottom, and a ladder going up into the hole. Painted on the outside of the egg was 'TM1'.

'Is that the time machine?' whispered Tony.

'Yes, it looks impressive, doesn't it?' said Dr P. 'But it doesn't work.'

'You can't give up hope, Dr P. It worked once, bringing you and your whole lab here, so there must be a way of fixing it,' said Tony.

Dr Polivoks sighed and sat down. He stroked his beard, then his head, and his beard again. As he did so, several Blue Bloos popped up from the floor and crowded round him, blooping. They began scratching their heads and imaginary beards.

Tony noticed all the clocks ticking away inside the shed. He became worried about how long he had been away from home, and from his ship the *Invincible*.

'Dr P, please can we get going on this?'

'Ahem, yes, right you are. Bleep. Bloop. Bluuurp.'

And a crowd of Blue Bloos slid and
bounced up into the air, forming themselves
into a blue board.

Dr P produced a piece of chalk from his
top pocket.

'Right. So THIS is the problem,' he said.

'We are HERE. But we want to be HERE.

'And this is the space-time continuum and
this is the stable-cheese regularity factor …'

Dr P began making funny marks on the blackboard, muttering to himself, occasionally getting a mini-computer-thing out of his pocket, tapping at it, muttering and doing more scribbling.

'Until …

'Finally …

'So the answer is … CHEESE.

'QED; quod erat demonstrandum,' said Dr P.

'I'm sorry, I don't follow,' said Tony.

'I've done these calculations before and it always comes down to the same thing,' said Dr P.

'The Cheese. What sort of cheese was it? How much of it was there? We simply need to get enough of the right type of cheese. Place it in my atomiser-bulb-array and the time machine will work, and we simply move this arrow forward, type in the date we want to get to and we will be back in our future.'

'OK, great. So where we can we get some cheese?'

'That's the problem, Tony, there isn't *any* in

this dimension.' Dr Polivoks sighed. 'I'm sorry, I really am not a very good scientist. Nothing I ever do works out properly.'

'Well, I think you're a very good scientist. I mean, look at all these things you've made. Blue Bloo City, the Blue Bloos and all the things in here. Like this,' ventured Tony, pointing to a large horn. 'Or this, what's this?'

'Oh, that. That's my communiscope.'

'What does it do?'

'It should allow you to communicate with anyone, anywhere.'

'Does it work?'

'A bit,' replied Dr P.

Tony thought hard. 'Dr P, can we use it to

communicate with our universe, with my home

for example?'

'Well, probably, where do you live?'

'Twenty-seven Winter Road, Felpham,

Britain, planet Earth.'

11. THE COMMUNISCOPE

Huffing and puffing though his beard, Dr Polivoks stood in front of the machine, flicked a few switches and then began to adjust some dials. As he did so, a small glow appeared in the middle of the screen, gradually growing sharper and brighter until it broke up into a light and dark pattern. It showed Tony's street.

'Dr Polivoks, I thought you said your

inventions never worked. This communiscope
thing seems to work perfectly. That's my house!
Can you zoom in, so I can see it better?'

'Yes, you twist this here, and push this
here.'

The dots on the screen gradually began to form the image of a front door. There was a girl standing on the doorstep, knocking.

'It's Chandra! She's arriving at my house for tea, but I'm not there.'

The girl knocked again, waited, and then the door opened to reveal a woman holding a baby.

'It's my mum and Tara!' exclaimed Tony. 'They're closing the door – can we follow them in? I need to see what happens next.'

'Of course. You just twist this, push this.'

'Mum's saying something. I think she's wondering where I am. This is not good, not good at all,' said Tony.

Suddenly Chandra noticed something on the carpet and picked it up. It was Tony's communicator. She showed it to Tony's mum.

'Dr P, this is awful.'

'Yes, I know. It was meant to be a two-way thing … but it isn't. You see, we can see them, but they can't see us. And the sound only works one way too.'

'The sound? It has sound?'

'Yes, we can't hear them, but they can hear us. Watch this.'

Dr Polivoks grabbed a round spongy thing, pulled it towards his mouth and bellowed, 'HELLOO!'

The effect was instantaneous. To start with everyone in the room looked shocked, then they looked at each other and started to laugh, and began crowding round Tara.

'They think that was Tara,' exclaimed Tony.

Somehow we need to get a message back to our universe, thought Tony. *We need to tell them where I am, and tell them to help us fix this machine, so I can get home. But who can I trust?*

12. WHO YA GONNA CALL?

When Tony's mum walked out of the room with Tara, leaving Chandra alone in the lounge, Tony seized his chance and whispered softly into the microphone.

'Chandra.' He spoke quietly, so as not to alarm her. 'Chandra, Chandra, can you hear me? It's me, Tony.'

Chandra started to look around the room,

behind the sofa, behind the door, and was
looking confused.

'Ahh, good, you can hear me. Listen, I need your help.'

Tony continued, 'Now, don't worry. I'm just stuck. In another dimension. I need your help to get back home.'

Chandra said something else. Tony hoped it was 'yes'.

'Thank you! Listen, my watch, my communicator, it's in your hand. I need that, and … a piece of cheese, or rather as much cheese as you can get.'

Tony could see Chandra's face looking a bit confused again so he said the next bit quickly.

'Then I need you to put all the cheese beside my communicator on Tara's round playmat. And I need you to leave the room.

When you come back into the room, the cheese and the communicator will be gone … I know it sounds really weird, but please trust me.

'I can tell you all about it afterwards, but right now I need you to trust me. If it all goes to plan I'll be back a couple of minutes after that.'

Tony watched Chandra's face closely, trying to work out what she was thinking.

'My goodness, Tony, I do believe you have a good friend there. Look she's walking to the kitchen, over to the fridge. She's going to do it. Brilliant, brilliant! Now, how do you suppose we are going to get all that stuff back here?' said Dr P.

'By teleportation! My spaceship has a teleporter on it, Dr Polivoks, and the coordinates are locked to that playmat. My spaceship can teleport it all back, then we can mend the time machine with the cheese, and all travel back to our universe together!'

'What a clever chap you are. I'm so glad you dropped by! Now, this spaceship of yours, where is it? It would seem we'll have to get to that quite quickly. Chandra has already got armfuls of cheese from your fridge.'

'It's near where you were picking plants, Dr P. Where I first met you.'

'Ahh. Oh dear. Oh deary, deary me. I'm afraid this could be a problem. You see, here, if you put something down somewhere, it might not be there when you get back. It might be somewhere different. Things sort of move about here. On their own. Blue Bloo city is so big I can usually find it again, but a spaceship we might not find again for years!'

'But I haven't got years, I've just told Chandra to put the cheese and the communicator on the mat. We've got to find my ship!'

'Well, perhaps it's under here, or on top of here …'

'Professor, it's a SPACESHIP. It's not going to be on your bookshelf!'

'Grr, I wish that fly would just buzz off!'
Dr P said.

Something buzzed past Tony's ear too. It
sounded a bit like a high-pitched mosquito.

'Concentrate, Dr P – please! Look, Chandra has come back from the kitchen with the cheese.'

'Oh yes, there's Stilton, and that looks like Camembert, or is it Brie?'

'Dr P, remember we need to find my spaceship!'

'Sorry, yes, maybe it's in this little cupboard …'

'Wait, Dr P. You've given me an idea.'

'What's that, Tony?'

'We've got to catch that fly.'

'You're telling me,' replied Dr P as he swished at it with a radar antenna.

And as it passed by Tony's head, he took three giant leaps up and cupped his hands, catching it between them.

Carefully stepping back down to the laboratory floor, Tony opened his hands and there, cupped between them, was a tiny miniature spaceship.

The *Invincible*!

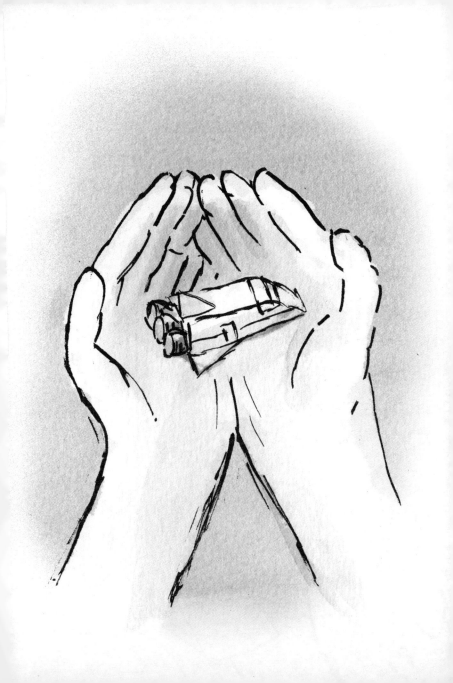

13. ANOTHER FINE MESS

On the communiscope, Tony could see that Chandra had come back into the lounge, and was about to place the cheese on the mat. There was no time to lose!

Dr P had begun to scribble notes furiously, saying things like, 'Fascinating. This gives me an idea. Yes, perhaps if I—'

Tony chose to ignore him. He was going to have to do this by himself.

'Computer, Computer, can you hear me?'

Pressing his ear close to the tiny spaceship, Tony could just hear it respond.

'Affirmative, Tony. I have been following you in miniature form since I lost visual contact.

'I still have the coordinates of the playmat in your house and can attempt teleportation at your command, though I have to warn you, Tony, it might not work, nobody has ever tried this before—'

'I know, but we have to try.'

Tony could see Chandra carefully putting his communicator beside a big pile of cheese on Tara's playmat.

'Computer, are you ready? Teleport …

NOW!'

But just at the moment Tony said, 'NOW!' the kitchen door flew open as baby Tara crawled into the lounge at top speed, grabbing the communicator. Chandra lunged to grab Tara but knocked the communicator across the floor.

And then FLASH! The cheese, Chandra and Tara were gone ...

… reappearing on the floor of Dr

Polivoks's laboratory.

When Tony saw Chandra with Tara his jaw nearly hit the floor.

As soon as Tara saw Tony she burbled, 'Gagg gagg!'

Chandra didn't say anything.

The doctor looked up from his calculations and saw the pile of cheese.

'Cheese, oooh, cheese! Look at all that lovely smelly cheese,' he said.

And then Tara, in an effort to pull herself upright, grabbed handfuls of cables that were across the floor.

Although she was small, she was strong. She managed to haul herself upright so she could wobbly-stand like her big brother and the funny man, causing the cables to move and the giant silver egg to rock, topple and then fall with a crash, sending little bits everywhere.

14. THE OTHER
WAY ROUND

Tara started crying, so Tony picked her up to soothe her. 'Oh my, whatever will we do now?'

Chandra couldn't quite seem to get any words out either.

'Tony – I – But –'

The Blue Bloos crowded around them and began bleeping.

'BOOOOOOOO! HOOOOOOO!'

As soon as Tara saw them she began to
giggle. Tony loved it when she giggled. Tony
didn't know quite what to say either, but seeing
Tara giggle made him feel a bit giggly too. Very
soon Chandra began to join in.

On the floor were bits of the Time Machine™ and the atomiser-air-bulb-array. Dr Polivoks was staring at it, transfixed.

He picked it up and inspected it closely. The outside of it was bent, causing the insides to be twisted into hundreds of different connections.

Then he smiled, and he started giggling too, soon turning into a full-blown belly laugh.

'Ha ha ha, I don't believe it! I've just been looking at this the wrong way round. Yes, sometimes you have to see things from another perspective.'

'What do you mean?'

Dr Polivoks was at the blueboard again, scribbling furiously. As he worked he talked.

'Tony, you want to get home, right?'

'Yes!'

'Chandra, you want to get home, right?'

'Um … yes?'

'Yes, of course you do! And Tara, you want to get home, right?'

'Gaa.'

'Yes, of course you do! Well, I know how to do it, but we have to do it quickly.'

Looking at his mum's face on the communiscope, Tony would have to agree.

'Blue Bloo, pass me a quantimator please … Blep blep.'

'Blep blurp.'

'You see, Tony, you were right. Sometimes

you've got to make mistakes, try things out, suck it and see, as they say.'

'Did I say that?'

'Yes, but the important bit is not to get downhearted if it doesn't work out the way you hoped. Take your baby sister, Tina.'

'She's called Tara.'

'Yes, Tina, nice to finally meet you by the way. Take Tina for example. Imagine she sees a red wooden block. She might pick it up thinking it's food, like a nice shiny rosy apple. But chewing it doesn't taste nice. Does she get downhearted and cry?'

'Well, she might—'

'No, she doesn't,' Dr P continued. 'She's learnt that blocks don't taste nice, and next time she finds a red block she won't try to eat it. You see?'

'No, not really.' said Tony.

'And Chandra. You believed in Tony, you trusted him, you knew he needed help.'

Chandra nodded and said, 'You know, Tony, I always knew there was something different about you. You are going to explain all this to me, one day, when we get home, aren't you?'

'Yes, of course. It's all to do with my communicator, my spaceship and little Tara here. You see I have my own spaceship, it's called—'

'No time for explanations now,' interrupted Dr P. 'For now it's all about the cheese, the atomiser-air-bulb-array, and the Time Machine™. I know how it all fits together. I know how to get us back to the future!

'But I'll need your help, Tony, Chandra, and yours too, Tina.

'Are you ready?'

'Yes,' shouted Tony and Chandra in unison.

'Gaa,' shouted Tara.

On the communiscope Tony could see his mum and Chris. They were looking behind

sofas and doors, upstairs, downstairs, in the
back yard, all over the house, trying to find
Tony, Chandra and Tara.

'Right, hold this, please.

'Carry this, please.

'Chew this, please.'

Until finally ...

'We've done it!' exclaimed Dr P.

'Right, in you go, quickly, the countdown has begun. There are seat belts for all of you. Make sure you strap yourselves in. I've set the coordinates for twenty-seven Winter Road. And don't worry, everything will work out just fine. Hopefully.'

'But wait, Dr Polivoks, what about you, aren't you coming with us?' asked Tony.

'I'm afraid not, Tony. I've thought long and hard about it, and this is where I belong now. I'm old and it would be too hard for me to relearn everything so this is where I'll stay.

'Besides, this spaceship of yours, the teleporter, your communicator, they have given me lots of ideas. Enough work to keep me and my Blue Bloo friends busy for years.

'And don't worry; now I've got plenty of cheese, and my Time Machine™ fixed, so I can always come and visit some day.'

'I'd like that, Dr P. Remember: twenty-seven Winter Road, Planet Earth.'

'I will, I will … Goodbye Tony, goodbye Chandra, goodbye Tara! And thank you for your company!'

When Tara heard her name she held up her
hand to wave, 'Gye Gye.'

And they were gone.

15. HOME AGAIN

Travelling in the Time Machine™ was surprisingly smooth. Inside, they could see a clock whizzing round and round.

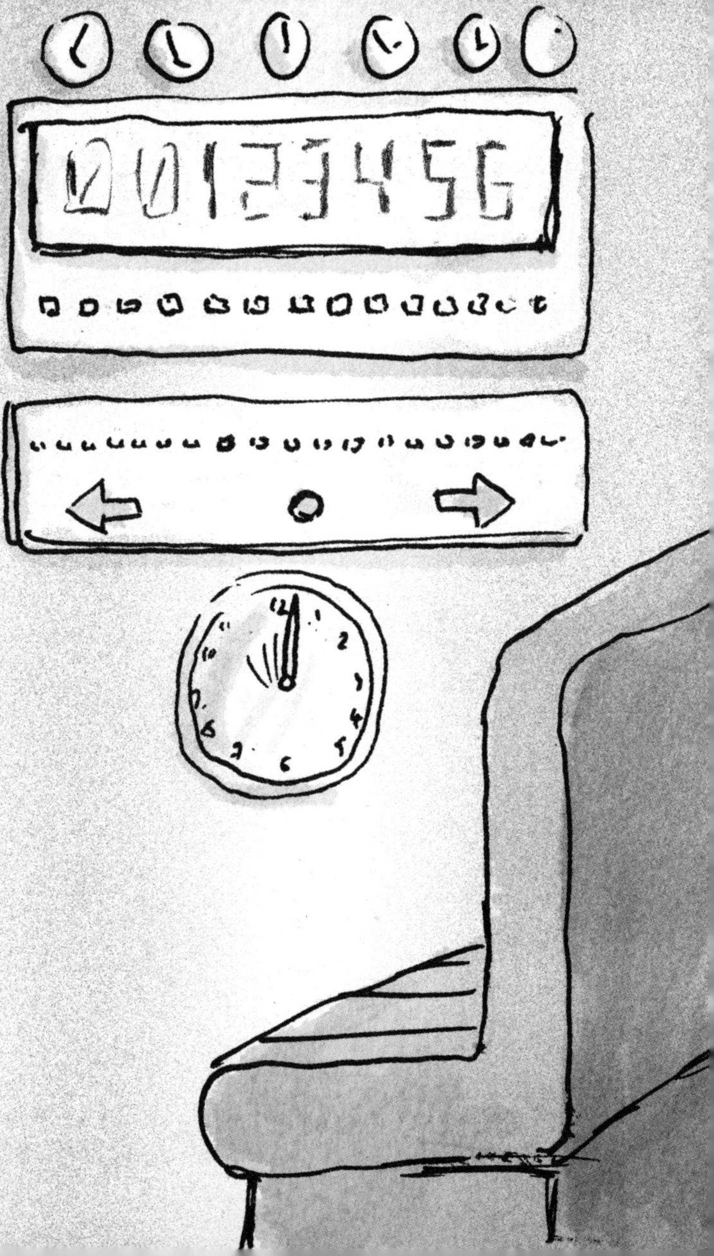

Outside, through the open door, silvery patterns shot by, until the motion seemed to stop, and the scene outside began to appear real and focused. Tony could see his lounge.

'Looks like our stop,' said Tony. 'I guess this is where we get out.'

Chandra clambered down the short ladder to the carpet. Tony followed with Tara in his arms. Then with a click-ping noise, the Time Machine™, Chandra and Tara were gone.

Tony looked around. He hadn't expected that to happen. He was alone again; there were

toys everywhere. There was his moon rocket model, still in one piece, on the floor beside Tara's toys. He picked it up and put it safely on top of the bookshelf, beside the clock, which said 4.15 p.m. He looked at his wrist. His communicator was on it, but the strap wasn't done up properly.

The house seemed quiet, very quiet. He fastened the strap on his communicator and walked into the kitchen. Where was everybody?

There was the cupboard where the button was hidden. Tony decided to check it. He opened the cupboard, moved some nappies to one side ... yes, there it was, the button.

All of a sudden the kitchen door flew open.

'WAHH WAHH WAHH.'

It was Mum. 'Ahh, Tony, brilliant. You must have known — what a good big brother you are! Throw me another pack of nappies, will you?'

'Tara, Mum, where have you been? I've missed you.'

'We've just been upstairs, Tony. I thought Tara needed a nap.'

'Ahh, Tara, you brave little adventurer, you,' said Tony, tickling Tara's tummy.

Tara looked at Tony and giggled.

'Ga ga.'

'What a sweet thing to say, Tony. And

listen,' continued his mum. 'Chandra will be here soon, so why don't you go and tidy Tara's toys in the lounge. They seem to be everywhere again.'

'Sure thing, Mum.'

And he was off.

EPILOGUE

Tony was overjoyed to see Chandra later that evening.

And Tony's mum was making beans and double cheese on toast.

'Right, that's the beans and the toast. Just the cheese now and I've got lots in the fridge. Oh? That's funny, where did I put it? Oh dear. I'm sure it was here earlier.'

'I've got some cheese, Mrs Spears. Here in my pocket.'

'Have you, Chandra? Thank you very much, what a funny thing to have in your pocket!'

Chandra looked confused. 'Yes, I'm not sure why I brought it. Perhaps I knew you needed some?'

'The things you children keep in your pockets!'

Tony took his first mouthful and almost choked. He could feel the *Invincible* still in *his* pocket, miniaturised.

Tara was sitting at the table too, in her high chair. She was having yoghurt with pieces of cucumber, though most of it seemed to be landing in her bib.

'Ga ga.'

After tea Tony and Chandra got down to play.

'Tony,' said Chandra.

'Um, yeah.'

'You know what? I had the weirdest dream the other day. I dreamt that you had a spaceship, not a toy one, a real one. Isn't that strange?'

And suddenly Chandra's look changed, and she looked at him quite directly, with a quizzical smile.

'Tony, if you really did have your own spaceship, you would tell me, wouldn't you?'

'Um, yes. Of course … '

'Good, that's what I thought.'

'Chandra—' Tony began.

BRRRRRRRRRRRRRRRING!

'Oh crumbs, that's my dad, he must have come early to pick me up,' said Chandra. 'What was it you were going to say, Tony?'

'Um, you'd better go. See you later, Chandra …we can talk more tomorrow at school, right?'

'About spaceships?'

'Yeah, I've got something I'd like to show you …'

Tony checked his pocket. The *Invincible* was still there – the perfect size for his school bag.